D0210772

# Dear Parents:

Congratulations! Your child is taking the first steps on an exciting journey. The destination? Independent reading!

**STEP INTO READING®** will help your child get there. The program offers five steps to reading success. Each step includes fun stories and colorful art or photographs. In addition to original fiction and books with favorite characters, there are Step into Reading Non-Fiction Readers, Phonics Readers and Boxed Sets, Sticker Readers, and Comic Readers—a complete literacy program with something to interest every child.

## Learning to Read, Step by Step!

**Ready to Read   Preschool–Kindergarten**
• big type and easy words • rhyme and rhythm • picture clues
For children who know the alphabet and are eager to begin reading.

**Reading with Help   Preschool–Grade 1**
• basic vocabulary • short sentences • simple stories
For children who recognize familiar words and sound out new words with help.

**Reading on Your Own   Grades 1–3**
• engaging characters • easy-to-follow plots • popular topics
For children who are ready to read on their own.

**Reading Paragraphs   Grades 2–3**
• challenging vocabulary • short paragraphs • exciting stories
For newly independent readers who read simple sentences with confidence.

**Ready for Chapters   Grades 2–4**
• chapters • longer paragraphs • full-color art
For children who want to take the plunge into chapter books but still like colorful pictures.

**STEP INTO READING®** is designed to give every child a successful reading experience. The grade levels are only guides; children will progress through the steps at their own speed, developing confidence in their reading. The F&P Text Level on the back cover serves as another tool to help you choose the right book for your child.

Remember, a lifetime love of reading starts with a single step!

*To Dr. Huddle, my personal Tooth Fairy*
*—C.R.*

*To my husband and Jeanette.*
*Thank you for always believing in me!*
*—M.D.*

Text copyright © 2017 by Candice Ransom
Cover art and interior illustrations copyright © 2017 by Monique Dong
All rights reserved. Published in the United States by Random House Children's Books,
a division of Penguin Random House LLC, New York.
Step into Reading, Random House, and the Random House colophon are registered
trademarks of Penguin Random House LLC.

Visit us on the Web!
StepIntoReading.com
randomhousekids.com

Educators and librarians, for a variety of teaching tools, visit us at
RHTeachersLibrarians.com

Library of Congress Cataloging-in-Publication Data is available upon request.

ISBN 978-0-399-55364-6 (trade) — ISBN 978-0-399-55365-3 (lib. bdg.) —
ISBN 978-0-399-55366-0 (ebook)

Printed in the United States of America
10 9 8 7 6 5 4 3 2 1

This book has been officially leveled by using the F&P Text Level
Gradient™ Leveling System.

# Tooth Fairy's Night

by Candice Ransom

illustrated by Monique Dong

Random House 🏠 New York

Day is over.
Moon is low.

Wake up,
Tooth Fairy!
Time to go!

Money,
lunch box,
address book.

# Fill the pet bowl.

# One last look.

# First stop–
# this house!

# Zip below.

Open window.

Shhh!

Tip-toe!

Under pillow,

two teeth?

Three!

Drop the coins
and wiggle free.

Next stop—uh-oh!
Puppy dog.

Use the sleep dust!

Out like a log.

First tooth fell out!

Hop for joy.

# Happy dance for
# the lucky boy.

Dark sky,
bright stars—
time for a break.

Pour the tea
and cut the cake.

# Under covers,
# green cat eyes.

# Fast paw—too slow!

# Big surprise!

# Bears and bunnies,
# what a zoo!

So many toys—
must get through.

So many teeth.
Push and pull.

Hard to fly
with tooth bag full!

Over tree tops,
see the sun.

Time to fly home.

Work is done.

# Brush and floss.

# Turn out the light.

Kick off slippers.

Nighty-night!